# New Canaan Library
**151 Main Street**
**New Canaan, CT  06840**

(203) 594-5000
www.newcanaanlibrary.org

This Swiss-Italian story is almost 150 years old and comes from Canton Ticino in southern Switzerland. Originally preserved orally, the author found it in a book of local folklore from the region.

Copyright © 2006 by NordSüd Verlag AG, Gossau Zürich, Switzerland
First published under the title *So ein Sausen ist in der Luft* by Ravensburger.
Published in Switzerland under the title *Die Nacht im Zauberwald*

English translation copyright © 2006 by North-South Books Inc., New York.

First published in the United States, Great Britain, Canada, Australia, and New Zealand in 2006 by North-South Books Inc., an imprint of NordSüd Verlag AG, Gossau Zürich, Switzerland. Distributed in the United States by North-South Books Inc., New York.

Library of Congress Cataloging-in-Publication Data is available.
A CIP catalogue record for this book is available from The British Library.

ISBN-13: 978-0-7358-2102-6 / ISBN-10: 0-7358-2102-X (trade edition)
10 9 8 7 6 5 4 3 2 1

Printed in Belgium

# A TALE OF TWO BROTHERS

By Eveline Hasler
Illustrated by Käthi Bhend
Translated by Marianne Martens

NORTHSOUTH
BOOKS
New York · London

Once upon a time, long, long ago, there lived two brothers. Their names were Morris and Boris. They looked like twins since they both had humps on their backs. From a distance, it looked as though they were carrying backpacks.

But if you got to know them, you'd see that they were very different. Morris was helpful and kind to everyone he met. He took care of the cattle and fussed over the plants in the garden.

But Boris never had a kind word for anyone. He beat the cows and never gave them quite enough to eat. The plants on his land grew wild, nearly choked by weeds.

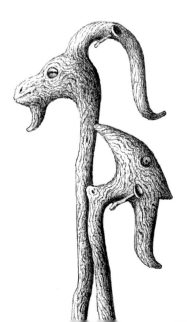

When fall came, Morris said to Boris, "It's time for one of us to go up the mountain. There are some shingles loose on the roof of our hut up there, and we'll need to fix them before the snow comes. I went in spring, so it's your turn."

"What, me?" shouted Boris. "I don't feel like it. It takes more than a day to get there."

Rather than arguing with his brother, Morris decided to just go himself.

He set out on the long journey.

The night before, a storm had ripped the last few leaves from the branches of the trees. Plump chestnuts were tucked between the leaves on the ground and when he stepped on them, they burst out of their prickly husks. Morris bent down and picked up as many as he could carry.

When Morris grew tired of climbing, he stopped for a snack. He sat on a tree stump and watched the ants running around.

"Don't worry, I won't hurt you," said Morris, taking some bread and cheese out of his bag.

By lunchtime he'd reached a high plateau. The path was overgrown with thorny branches. He struggled through, but thorns clung to his clothes and scratched his arms and legs. Patiently, he untangled the prickly tendrils, marveling at how intricate they were.

Soon he saw some mushrooms. Their red hats glowed merrily above their stems.

"Hello, toadstools," he said admiringly. "I know I can't eat you, but you sure do look lovely." They seemed to be growing in a secret circle.

The path dipped down into a ravine. This had always been his favorite point of the journey. If you shouted toward the cliff, it would echo back at you.

"Beautiful forest," shouted Morris. "Beautiful man-man-man-man," answered the echo. Morris thought he heard a giggle behind the branches, but he didn't see anyone.

A big toad was hiding in the shadows of the trees. Its moist skin was dirt-colored and covered with warts.

Morris bent down for a closer look and noticed what beautiful eyes the toad had. Golden irises encircled dark pupils.

Dusk fell, and Morris built a fire and roasted his chestnuts. They crackled in the heat and their roasted shells popped open. Their chalky middles were sweet and delicious. Morris stoked the fire and stretched out on the ground to rest. There were many sounds all around him and, spellbound, he listened to them in the darkness.

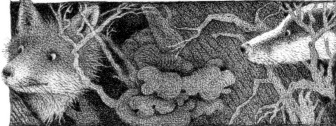

Where was that rattling sound coming from? Maybe a mouse, he thought. And what about that creaking sound in the woodpile? Must be a fox looking for his dinner, thought Morris. And what about that snorting? That had to be a badger. "I am safe here," said Morris quietly. "I can just close my eyes and go to sleep."

Morris had barely fallen asleep when strange figures crept out from behind trees to have a look at him.

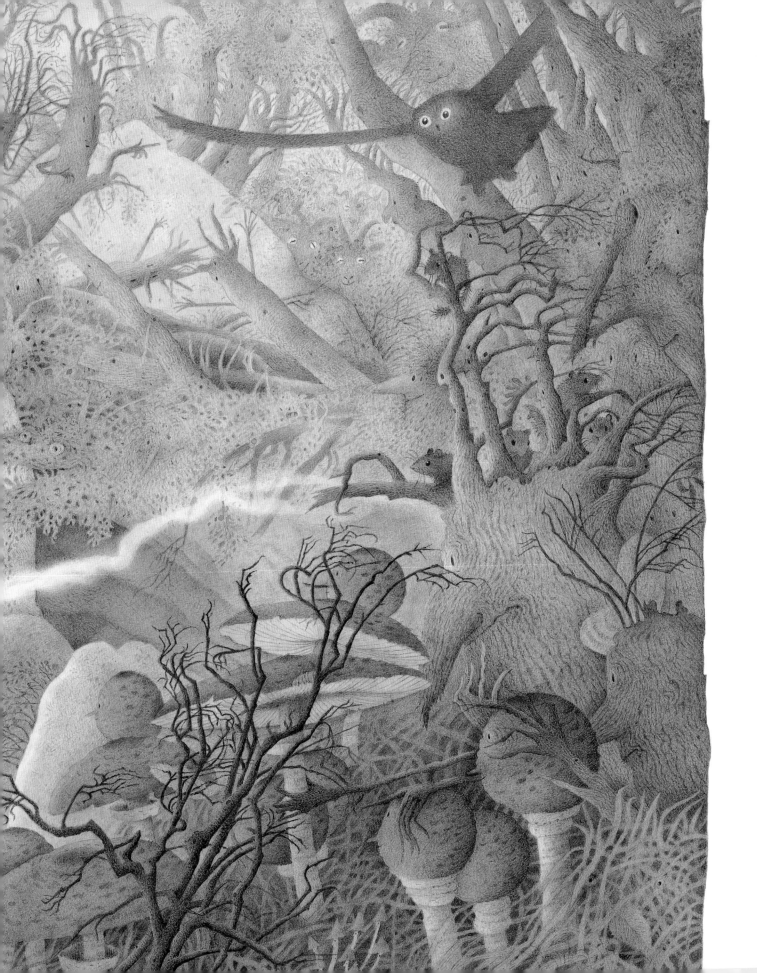

"It's a human! And he's on our land!"
said the roots. "What should we do with
him? Does anyone know him?"

"We know him," said the mushroom
creatures.

"We know him very well," said the
plant elves.

"We know him," said the tree spirits.
They whispered and discussed.

"Let's give him something that he
will never forget," said the forest witch
at last.

When Morris woke, it was dawn. He rubbed his eyes. What a noisy night that was, he thought as he stretched. Whistling happily, he went on his way up the mountain. Soon, he heard a stream. Water! Just what I need. He washed himself and saw his reflection in the water. He looked very cheerful. Must be from the blue sky, he thought.

At last Morris reached the hut.

Quickly, he got to work fixing the roof.

On his way home, Morris walked with big, swinging steps. He'd never felt so light and free. It was almost as if he were flying. Soon he arrived back home in the valley.

Boris was chopping wood in front of his house. He stared in shock at his brother. "Where's your hump?" he asked.

"My hump?" asked Morris, reaching over his shoulder. There was nothing there! The hump was gone!

What's good for my brother must also be good for me, thought Boris. So the next day, Boris set out, mindful to go the same way that Morris had gone.

He stopped for a snack in the same place his brother had stopped. On the plateau, he swatted angrily at the thorny bushes with his cane.

"Hey, you stinky old mushrooms," he shouted at the toadstools. Carelessly, he stomped on them.

But what goes around, comes around.

Boris was soon in the ravine. "What sorry old trees," shouted Boris at the cliff.

"What a sorry old man-man-man-man," shouted the echo back at him. It was almost as though someone was laughing at him.

Boris saw the toad, too. Luckily, at the very last minute, it managed to save itself from being squashed under his shoe.

"Out of my way, you ugly old cow pie," he shouted at it.

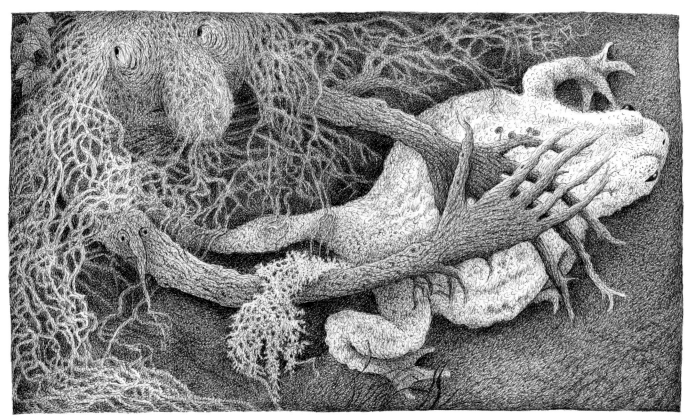

When it grew dark, Boris made a fire. "There aren't even any chestnut trees here," he thought angrily. "Only pine trees and birch trees. How useless. They have no fruits to cook." As the fire died down, Boris lay down and listened to the night. Where was that rattling sound coming from? he wondered fearfully. And what about that creaking sound in the woodpile? And what about that snorting sound? Feeling frightened, he sat up and threw rocks into the bushes. Then it grew quiet. The quiet was even scarier.

Finally he fell asleep. Strange figures came out of the bushes. They circled him.

"It's a human! And he's on our land!" said the roots. "What should we do with him? Does anyone know him?"

"We know him," said the mushroom creatures.

"We know him very well," said the plant elves.

"We know him," said the tree spirits.

They whispered and discussed.

"Let's give him something that he will never forget," said the forest witch at last.

The next morning when he woke up, Boris felt weary. He'd slept badly all night. Such strange noises he'd heard! The clouds hung low, as if snow were on the way. In a bad mood, he continued on his way. By the stream, he ate the last of his provisions and carelessly dumped his scraps in the water. When he saw his reflection in the water, it scared him. He had to remind himself that it was only a reflection. Surely the waves were distorting the image.

When he reached the hut, it started to snow. Boris took a short nap.

After all, he didn't have to fix the roof. His brother had already done it for him, he thought, chuckling to himself at how clever he was to get out of that job! Besides, it was going to be a long trip home trudging through the snow.

When he finally arrived back home, he saw his brother bringing the goats into the stall. "How do I look?" he asked Morris.

Morris stared at his brother. He couldn't even speak—Boris's hump was bigger than ever!

Sadly Boris whistled for his dog. "Why, oh why, did this happen to me?" he asked the dog. Boris lifted his hand as if to pet the dog for the first time, but the dog ducked fearfully, bared his teeth, growled, and ran away. Suddenly Boris realized something.

Boris understood that the difference between his brother's trip and his trip lay within himself. "I'm going to take the trip again," he said. "Not now. Not in the snow. But in the spring."